PIRATE SCHOOL
Camp Buccaneer

by Brian James
illustrated by Jennifer Zivoin

Grosset & Dunlap

For my best friend Dan.—BJ

To Aunty Linda, Uncle Chris, Amanda, and Emily, for all the great summers at "Camp Mello."— JZ

GROSSET & DUNLAP
Published by the Penguin Group
Penguin Group (USA) Inc., 375 Hudson Street, New York, New York 10014, USA
Penguin Group (Canada), 90 Eglinton Avenue East, Suite 700,
Toronto, Ontario M4P 2Y3, Canada
(a division of Pearson Penguin Canada Inc.)
Penguin Books Ltd., 80 Strand, London WC2R 0RL, England
Penguin Group Ireland, 25 St. Stephen's Green, Dublin 2, Ireland
(a division of Penguin Books Ltd.)
Penguin Group (Australia), 250 Camberwell Road, Camberwell, Victoria 3124, Australia
(a division of Pearson Australia Group Pty. Ltd.)
Penguin Books India Pvt. Ltd., 11 Community Centre,
Panchsheel Park, New Delhi—110 017, India
Penguin Group (NZ), 67 Apollo Drive, Rosedale, North Shore 0632, New Zealand
(a division of Pearson New Zealand Ltd.)
Penguin Books (South Africa) (Pty.) Ltd., 24 Sturdee Avenue,
Rosebank, Johannesburg 2196, South Africa

Penguin Books Ltd., Registered Offices:
80 Strand, London WC2R 0RL, England

Library of Congress Cataloging-in-Publication Data is available.

ISBN 978-0-448-44865-7   10 9 8 7 6 5 4 3 2

Chapter 1
Grimy Guts!

"Yucky blucky!" Inna groaned. She held a rotten fishtail in one hand and pinched her nose closed with the other.

"Aye! You can say that again," I told her. I didn't even get to pinch my nose. I had both hands full of fish stink.

The stink was starting to make me the teeniest bit seasick. Only pirates aren't supposed to get seasick, not even pirate kids like us. So I did my best to hide it and I kept working.

"Arrr! This is the worst job Rotten Tooth has ever made us do!" Vicky complained as she mopped up the drippy bits of fish guts.

"AYE! You can say that again, too!" I said.

Since we'd been aboard the *Sea Rat* for Pirate School, Rotten Tooth had made us do a lot of nasty chores, but cleaning the fish gut tank was absolutely, positively the worst!

Rotten Tooth was the ship's first mate. He was also the meanest, cruelest pirate who ever sailed the seas. And to make things worse, he was our teacher and he didn't like us pirate kids one little bit!

"Aye, that Rotten Tooth sure can be a grouchy beard sometimes," I said.

Just then, Aaron poked his head up. He was inside the tank. He was covered from head to toe in smelly, slimy gunk! His job was to toss all the bones and gross gunk onto the deck so the rest of us could throw it overboard.

One look at him made me feel icky sicky all over.

"Blimey!" he shouted. "Rotten Tooth is *always* a grouchy beard!"

Vicky glared at him.

"ARRR! Maybe he wouldn't be so grouchy if *you* weren't so daft all the time!" Vicky shouted back at him. Her dark eyes looked even darker whenever she was mad. Vicky was Aaron's twin sister and she thought he was a big fat show-off. "You're always getting us into trouble!" she told him.

"Am not!" Aaron shouted.

"Are too!" Vicky barked. "We wouldn't be cleaning this stinky tank if you hadn't tied Rotten Tooth's beard into a knot!"

It was a true fact.

Rotten Tooth snored through our whole entire pirate lesson this morning. So Aaron tied the two pointy ends of his green beard into a knot.

I started to giggle when I remembered how steamed Rotten Tooth got. "It was pretty funny," I mumbled.

Aaron smiled.

Then Vicky glared at me.

I covered my mouth real quick.

"Arrr, it's not funny, Pete!" Inna hollered at me. Inna didn't think anything was funny if it ended with us getting dirty. That's because she was the only pirate kid in the whole wide world who liked to stay squeaky clean and wear fancy clothes.

"Aye!" Vicky agreed. "We have to spend our entire recess cleaning up this mess and it's all Aaron's fault!"

"Quit bellyaching!" Aaron said. "It won't take that long. Once Gary comes back with those buckets, this job will be easy breezy! We'll have these guts scooped out in no time."

"Aye," I said. Then I scratched my head and looked around the deck. "Where is Gary, anyway?" I asked.

Gary was my best mate at Pirate School. We both had light-colored hair and wore shipshape pirate hats. Only Gary wore glasses and was almost a whole year younger than me. Plus, he was just the tiniest bit clumsy. But besides all of those things, we were exactly alike.

"Avast! Here he comes," Vicky said, pointing across the deck. I couldn't see Gary's head. He was completely hidden behind a stack of buckets that wibbled and wobbled as he walked.

"Ahoy, mates!" Gary shouted as he got closer.

"Ahoy right back," I said.

Just then, the stack of buckets started to wibble and wobble even more. That's because Gary stepped right into a slippery puddle of goo!

My mouth dropped open!

"Uh-oh," I said.

Gary slipped and slid across the deck. Then . . . *BOOM!*

He crashed right into Inna! They both fell smack into a pile of fish bones that Aaron had tossed out.

Inna's face turned bright red.

"Double uh-oh," Vicky whispered to me.

Inna reached up and pulled a fish bone out of her hair. "Ewwwww! Gross!" she

wailed. Then she stood up and grabbed
Gary's hat. She pulled it down over his ears
and bopped him on the head. "ARRR! YOU
ARE SUCH A BLUNDER HEAD!" she
shouted.

"Arrr, I'm sorry," Gary mumbled as he
fixed his hat. "I never blunder on purpose."

I thought for sure Inna was going to
toss Gary overboard. But just then Captain
Stinky Beard came out of his quarters and
marched over to us. We forgot all about the
fishy business and gave him a real pirate
salute.

"Ahoy, me lil' shipmates," Captain Stinky Beard bellowed. Then he gave us a real big smile when he saw how messy we were. "Ye lot look to be having fun," he said.

Inna folded her arms and made a huff.

The rest of us nodded our heads and smiled. We didn't want the cap'n to know we were being punished. Because even though Rotten Tooth was a grouchy beard, he was still our teacher and Captain Stinky Beard didn't like it when we made him mad.

"Arrr, I just came to tell ye that we've set sail for Camp Buccaneer," Captain Stinky Beard told us. "Ye mates have been working hard and you deserve to have some fun!"

"Aye aye!" we shouted.

Then we jumped up and down. Even Inna wasn't gloomy anymore. After putting up with all of Rotten Tooth's rotten chores, we couldn't wait to get to camp!

Chapter 2
Camp Rules!

"Yo ho ho! Camp Buccaneer!" I cheered once Captain Stinky Beard had left. "I can't even believe it! This is the best thing ever."

"Aye," Gary agreed. Then he scratched his head. "Only one thing, Pete?" he asked. "What's Camp Buccaneer?"

My mouth dropped open and I made a surprised face.

"Great sails!" I cried. "Camp Buccaneer is where pirate kids from all over the seas go to see which kids are the most piratey!"

Gary wrinkled his nose and scratched his head again. He always does that when his brain is confused. "But Pete, how do they know who the most piratey kids are?" he asked.

Aaron folded his arms and lifted his chin in the air. Vicky called that his know-it-all face.

"Blimey! Everyone knows that," Aaron said.

Vicky leaned against the ship's mast and gave Aaron a mean look. "Arrr, *you* don't know!" she said.

"How do you know?" Aaron asked.

"Because," Vicky argued, "I've never heard of Camp Buccaneer, either. And that means *you've* never heard of it."

That was a true fact. Since Vicky and Aaron were twins, they'd spent every day of their lives together. So if Vicky didn't know something, then Aaron couldn't know it, either. That's one of the rules of being a twin.

"Hogwash! I know all about it," Aaron said. He marched away and grabbed a fishing pole that was leaning against the railing. Then he jumped around and swung it over his head like a sword. "We swashbuckle until the last kid is standing!

That's how they know who the most piratey is!"

I ducked my head just as the fishing pole swished above me.

"Swashbuckling is only one of the competitions," I said, grabbing the pole. "There are sailing races, treasure hunts, and lots of other things, too."

"Aye?" Aaron asked. "We really get to swashbuckle?"

"Aye!" I said.

Vicky huffed. "I thought you knew all about Camp Buccaneer already," she teased Aaron.

I didn't want to see Aaron and Vicky fight anymore, so I quickly started to explain how the competition worked.

"On my old ship, the pirates used to tell me tales of when they went to Camp Buccaneer. The first place team in each game gets a bunch of points. The second place team gets some points. Third place gets less points. Any team after that place gets zero points. Then they add up all those points to figure out the winner."

"Arrr! That does sound like fun," Gary said.

"Aye, and that's not even the best part," I told them. "The best part is that the winning team gets a captain-sized treasure!"

"Aye?" Inna asked. "A real treasure with jewels and diamonds?"

"Aye!" I said.

Inna smiled and rubbed her hands together.

"Blow me down," Vicky said. "If we win that treasure, we'll be rich!"

"Aye," Aaron said. "We'll be richer than ol' Rotten Face! Then we can order *him* to clean the stinky fish tank!"

"AYE?" a voiced boomed behind us.

I spun around and GULPED!

Rotten Tooth was standing right there.

"What be all this talk about treasure?" he growled, showing us his sharp, green teeth. "AND BETTER YET, WHY AIN'T YE BARNACLES WORKING?" he roared.

We all DOUBLE GULPED!

Rotten Tooth looked very, very, super-angry. And even though we were brave pirate kids, none of us was brave enough to stand up to Rotten Tooth.

Well . . . almost none of us.

Inna marched right over to him and poked him in the belly with her finger. "Arrr, the cap'n told us to stop and pack our stuff," she said. "He said we're shipping out for Camp Buccaneer and his orders beat your orders, so there!"

I shook my head. I couldn't believe that Inna could be afraid of things like snakes and crabs but not Rotten Tooth, who was even meaner than a shark!

"Hmmm," Rotten Tooth mumbled. Then he tugged at his beard. I had to cover up a giggle when I noticed that there was still a tiny knot in it. "Well, orders be orders," he said. "At least I get ye pollywogs out of me hair for a few days."

"Arrr, too bad he can't get the stink out of his hair, too!" Vicky whispered to me.

We both went all giggly.

"ARRR!" Rotten Tooth sneered. We both covered our mouths real quick. "We can't get there quick enough for my taste," he snarled as he walked away.

For once, we all agreed with ol' Rotten Head.

Chapter 3
Aye Aye, Campers!

"Sink me! Camp is only two days long, so what do you need all that for?" Aaron asked Inna when she came above deck.

She was dragging two super-stuffed suitcases. The rest of us were only bringing tiny sacks with our toothbrushes and extra pairs of skivvies.

Inna folded her arms and lifted her chin high in the air.

"Arrr, I need one dress for sailing, one for treasure hunting, a bathing suit for swimming, and another outfit for swashbuckling," she said. "Plus, I need one really fancy dress for when we win. I want to look my best."

I rolled my eyes and shook my head.

Inna sure was one strange pirate kid!

"Arrr, do you really think we're going to win?" Gary asked.

"Great sails! Of course we are," Vicky answered.

"Aye," Aaron agreed. "No kids are better pirates than us!"

"Aye aye!" I said. "But all the kids invited to Camp Buccaneer are pretty good. So we still have to work hard," I warned my mates.

My friends nodded their heads.

Just then, we heard someone coming up behind us. It was Clegg! He was the oldest, wisest pirate on the *Sea Rat*. He was also our friend. He always told us the best tales.

"Ahoy, me lil' shipmates!" he said.

"Ahoy right back," I said.

"Off to Camp Buccaneer, are ye?" he asked. We nodded and smiled real wide. Then Clegg rubbed his eye patch. He only did that when he was remembering a good story. "I was at Camp Buccaneer myself when I was just a wee pirate like yourselves," he said.

"Aye?" we all asked in surprise.

"Aye!" Clegg answered.

"Did you win?" Aaron asked.

Clegg shook his head. "Arrr, me and my mates came in second place," he said.

"How come?" Vicky asked. "You're a great pirate!"

"Aye," the rest of us agreed.

Clegg smiled. "'Tis true," he said proudly. "But ye must beware of cheaters. Not every pirate follows all the rules of the pirate code," he warned.

I made a grumpy face.

"Gully fluff!" I groaned.

If there was one thing I didn't like, it was pirates who didn't follow the pirate code.

Clegg patted me on the head. "Arrr, just keep your eyes peeled and ye'll be okay," he said. Then he started to walk away. But he stopped real quick and turned around again. "Arrr, one last thing," he said. "Beware of the White Skeleton Monkey. Legend has it, he haunts the island and one bite will turn ye into a skeleton!"

Inna covered her ears. She didn't like to hear about spooky stuff.

The rest of us made *ooohhh*s and *aaahhh*s.

Then Clegg winked at us with his one good eye. "But don't worry too much. It hasn't been seen in a lifetime."

I wiped my forehead.

"Arrr, that was a close one," I said.

My friends all nodded their heads for the third time.

Then Clegg wished us luck and gave us a pirate salute. We all rushed to the railing on the deck and looked out to sea.

"AVAST!" I shouted when I spotted Camp Buccaneer. "Land ho!"

We were all so excited that we gave our pirate cheer.

"SWASHBUCKLING, SAILING, FINDING TREASURE, TOO! BECOMING PIRATES IS WHAT WE WANT TO DO!"

When we finished, we heard a booming laugh behind us. It was Rotten Tooth. We knew his laugh anywhere. It sounded worse than thunder during a sea storm!

"Arrr! What's so funny?" Inna growled.

"Ye lot thinking ye be real pirates, that's what." Rotten Tooth laughed. "You pollywogs will be lost without me holding your hands all the time."

"AYE?" I heard Captain Stinky Beard roar. I turned around and saw the captain standing behind us. And he didn't look happy. He didn't like it one bit when Rotten Tooth acted like a grouchy beard to us.

"Ummm . . . ahoy, C-Cap'n!" Rotten Tooth stuttered. "I was just reminding the little buckoes about all the lessons I've taught them at Pirate School."

"More like everything he didn't teach us," Vicky whispered.

Rotten Tooth snarled at her. She covered up her mouth real quick.

"Arrr, there be no need of that," Captain Stinky Beard finally said to Rotten Tooth.

"Aye? Why's that, Cap'n?" Rotten Tooth asked.

"Because *you* will be going with them," the cap'n ordered. "I'm ordering you to be their camp counselor!"

Rotten Tooth's mouth dropped open. "But Cap'n?" he pleaded, but Captain Stinky Beard waved him off. He said orders be orders and besides, he wanted the best pirate on the ship to go with us.

As we got ready to pull into port, Rotten Tooth grumbled more than ever. He hated camping! We couldn't help but giggle. Not only were we going to win the competition, but Rotten Tooth had to watch us do it! It served him right for teasing us.

Chapter 4
Dirty Scoundrels!

"Blow me down! Can't you do anything right?" Inna shouted.

"Sorry," Gary mumbled.

We were trying to set up our tent on the beach. Only it wasn't as easy as we thought. The wind kept blowing the tent away and Gary kept tripping over the ropes we were using to tie it down.

Rotten Tooth was supposed to help us, but he was nowhere in sight.

"Let's start over," I suggested.

I grabbed one corner of the tent. Vicky and Gary grabbed two other corners. Inna grabbed the last one and we were ready to tie them to the spikes. But just then, a real live monkey jumped down from the tree above us.

It landed smack down on Gary's head!

"SHIVER ME TIMBERS!" Gary screamed. "It's the White Skeleton Monkey!"

Inna covered her eyes and screeched. I held my breath, but then I saw that it wasn't the White Skeleton Monkey. It was just a plain old normal monkey. But Gary's glasses had been knocked off, so he couldn't see that.

"Steady up," I said. "It's just a normal monkey goofing around."

Gary put his glasses back on. "Oh, I knew that," he whispered. Inna gave him a dirty look. I thought for sure she was going to pull his hat down and bop him on the head again!

"Arrr, let's try this one more time," I said,

and we all grabbed onto the tent again.

"Blimey! You guys are doing it all wrong," Aaron said.

Vicky dropped her corner and crossed her arms.

"I don't see you helping, lazy guts!" she shouted.

"Gangway!" Aaron shouted. Then he pushed Vicky aside and grabbed ahold of the tent. "I can put it up all by myself!"

He quickly got hold of all four corners. Then he spun around really fast. The whole entire tent ballooned up into the air! We couldn't even see Aaron anymore.

By the time he was done, the tent was twisted around his tummy. Plus, Aaron had somehow pinned one of his pant legs into the ground with a spike.

"Way to go, Captain Big Mouth!" Vicky said.

Aaron made a grumpy face. "Okay, so I was wrong," he admitted. "Now, if you don't mind turning around, I need to step out of my pants."

We all started
to giggle and
turn around.
That's when I
saw two other
kids staring at
us. They were
pointing at us and laughing so hard that I
didn't feel giggly anymore.

"Avast! Those runts can't even pitch
their tent!" one of the kids roared.

"Aye, they might as well ship out before
the competition even starts," the other one
hollered back.

I marched right over to them. They
looked really mean. They were both bigger
than me, but I was no scallywag! I wasn't
going to let them get away with teasing my
mates.

"Arrr, we'll do just fine," I said. "We
might even win!"

"Aye," my friends shouted.

The two kids laughed even harder.

"Blimey, you can't win! Don't ye know

who we are?" the taller kid asked.

I shook my head.

"I'm Robert the Kid," he answered. "My dad is the dreaded Captain Black Heart Robert!"

"Arrr! And I be Two-Eyed Johnny, son of One-Eyed Johnny," the other kid said.

I gulped!

I knew all about them!

Black Heart Robert was captain of the *Dirty Waters*. He sank more ships than any other pirate captain! One-Eyed Johnny was his first mate. The pirates on my old ship said they were the rottenest pirates ever!

If Robert was even half as mean as his dad, we were in big trouble! So even though I was a brave pirate kid, my timbers started shaking and shivering just a teeny, tiny bit.

"Arrr, so ye heard of us?" Robert the Kid asked me.

I nodded my head up and down.

"Then ye also heard that we've won the last four Camp Buccaneer competitions?" Two-Eyed Johnny asked.

I DOUBLE GULPED!

"Arrr! So what!" Vicky shouted.

"Aye! You won't win this time," Aaron added. Then he tried to rush right up to them. Only his pants were still stuck, so he fell flat on his face!

Robert the Kid and Two-Eyed Johnny started to laugh all over again.

"Arrr! We're not afraid of any bullies!" Inna growled at them.

"Aye," Gary said.

"Aye aye!" I said. If my best mates weren't afraid, then neither was I.

"Come on, Johnny! Let's leave these shrimps," Robert the Kid said.

"Aye, we'll have plenty of time to laugh at them tomorrow when they're losing," Two-Eyed Johnny said.

Vicky stuck her tongue out at them as they walked away. The rest of us giggled. But on the inside, I could tell every one of us was worried that we might not win. Beating those bullies wasn't going to be easy.

Chapter 5
Let the Games Begin!

"Great sails! I didn't know there were this many pirate kids in the whole world," Gary said, looking around. All the teams had gathered on the beach for the start of the competition.

"Aye," I said. Only I wasn't looking at all the teams. I couldn't take my eyes off Robert the Kid and Two-Eyed Johnny. That was the team that really mattered.

As soon as the sun rose out of the sea,

Hook-Hand Edward shushed everyone up. He was the pirate in charge of Camp Buccaneer.

"Listen up, mateys!" he bellowed. Then he

explained the rules and told us which games we'd play in which order.

"Hooray!" Vicky cheered when Hook-Hand Edward announced that sailing would be the first race. "Me and Aaron are the best sailors around," she whispered. "We used to sail all the time when we lived on our old ship."

"If we win that, we'll be in good shape," I said.

We smiled real wide. Maybe it was going to be our lucky day.

"One last thing," Hook-Hand Edward warned. "Any rotten cheaters will be thrown out of camp!" Some of the other teams moaned and groaned. But I smiled. I wanted to win fair and square.

"Arrr, let's make haste," I said to my friends.

"Aye, time's a-wasting!" Aaron agreed.

"Aye," Inna said. "But first, I need to go change into my sailor outfit." Before any of us could argue, she ran toward our tent.

I slapped my head and rolled my eyes. I

wasn't so sure Inna understood what *racing* was all about.

The rest of us hurried over to the boats. We picked the best one we could find. Then Aaron and Vicky set up the sail. They didn't even fight.

I was testing the wind with my finger when Gary nudged me in the side.

"Uh-oh," he whispered. "Here comes trouble."

He was right. A whole bunch of stinky trouble was heading our way. That trouble was named Robert the Kid and Two-Eyed Johnny. They were in the boat right next to ours.

"Look who it is," Robert said when he saw me. "Peewee Pete and his gang."

I wrinkled up my nose and squinted my eyes. "We'll see who the peewee is when the race is over," I growled.

They started to laugh. Then Two-Eyed Johnny ducked down on the side of our boat. I remembered what Clegg told us about keeping our eyes peeled for cheaters.

Two-Eyed Johnny certainly looked like a cheater to me!

I was just about to go spy on him when Inna came running up in a fancy white sailor suit and hat with red ribbons.

"What are you supposed to be?" Robert asked her. "You don't look like any pirate I've ever seen." He laughed.

"Hmmmph!" Inna snorted. "Just because I like to look pretty doesn't mean I'm not a shipshape pirate," she told him. "And just because you're gross and mean doesn't make you a good pirate, either!"

"Arrr! We'll see about that!" Robert the Kid groaned.

I snuck away as they argued. I was just about to check on Two-Eyed Johnny when he popped his head up.

Then he and Robert both marched back to their own boat and left us alone.

"Arrr! Those two really ruffle my sails," I mumbled.

"Aye," Gary agreed, and we went back to work.

Soon it was time for the race to begin.

We all climbed into the boat and set sail. All of the other boats took off like sharks. Our boat was sailing smooth and steady. We were right there in the lead. But then we started to lose speed. Soon, we were crawling along like a sea turtle.

Vicky blamed Aaron.

"Blimey! You did something wrong," she shouted.

"Arrr, I did everything right!" Aaron shouted back. "Look, the wind is filling the sail just fine."

He was right. The sail was full. But *something* was wrong.

I reached under my pirate hat and scratched my head.

"Um . . . maybe this has something to

do with it," Gary said from the back of the boat.

We all turned around and looked at him. He was sitting down smack in a puddle of water!

We couldn't believe our eyes!

There was a hole in the side of our boat.

"Soggy sails! We've sprung a leak!" Vicky cried.

"Arrr! Or someone sprung it for us," I said. "Two-Eyed Johnny must have made the hole when we weren't paying attention. I knew those two scoundrels were up to no good!"

"Arrr, if they cheated, we can get them thrown out," Inna said.

"Aye," I said. "But we can't prove it."

"Aye," Aaron groaned.

"So what are we going to do now?" Vicky asked.

"There's only thing we can do," I said. "Me, Inna, and Gary will bail out the water. You and Aaron have to man the sails."

"Aye aye!" everyone shouted.

We started bailing out the water as fast as we could. Slowly, our boat started to pick up speed again. But we were already so far behind that there was no way we could catch up.

Chapter 6
Second Place Stinks!

We didn't win the sailboat race.

We didn't win the barrel toss, either.

Robert the Kid and Two-Eyed Johnny won them both.

Our team was down in the dumps as we headed for the last competition of the day.

"Arrr! It's not fair!" Inna complained. "They poked a hole in our boat and they filled our barrel with rocks instead of sand."

"Aye! Our barrel was heavier than everyone else's!" Vicky complained.

"Aye," Gary groaned. "We know those two rascals cheated and we can't even prove it!"

"Aye, but we're still almost in second place—that should make us feel proud," I said. I wasn't sure exactly what place we were in because I lost count of all the points. I was just trying to raise our spirits.

"Arrr! Second place stinks!" Aaron said.

"Aye! It stinks worse than Rotten Tooth's gruesome seaweed slop!" Inna moaned. Then she pinched her nose to show us all just how bad it stunk to be in second place.

"Arrr, maybe we can still win the next competition," I said.

My mates nodded. The last event of the day was a rope-climbing competition. We were shipshape climbers.

We looked up at the ropes dangling down from the trees. There was a landing platform in the trees to climb up to. Hook-Hand Edward said it was a test to show how well us pirate kids could scale the rigging on a ship.

"Arrr! That doesn't look so hard," Aaron said.

"Aye, we climb up to the crow's nest all the time," Vicky said. "We can do this!"

"Listen up, mateys!" Hook-Hand

Edward shouted to the crowd. "This here is a relay race. Each team member climbs to the platform. Then the next pirate  climbs up. Teams with only two and three kids need to pair up. Every team needs five members."

I counted our team. I was pretty sure we had five, but I counted a few more times just to make sure.

"Arrr, we're all set," I said once I was certain.

"I should climb first," Aaron said. "That way, we can build up a good lead."

"I'll climb second," Vicky said. "Then we'll have a bigger lead!"

"I'll go last," Gary said. "I might need the head start."

"Aye," we all agreed. Gary was better at falling than climbing.

Once the race started, everything went according to the plan. Aaron and Vicky climbed like the wind. I went next. I climbed as fast as I could. We still had a lead when Inna started to climb the rope.

She was halfway up when Gary pointed up from the ground and screamed.

"WHITE SKELETON MONKEY!" he hollered.

His hollering scared Inna out of her wits! She was so scared that she forgot to hold on to the rope and covered her eyes with both hands.

Then . . .

SPLASH!

Inna plopped down right into a mud puddle. The mud splattered

all over her pretty green dress. Some of it even splashed in her hair! Then she looked all around. "YOU BLUNDERER! LOOK WHAT YOU DID! THAT'S NOT THE WHITE SKELETON MONKEY. IT'S A CLOUD!"

She rushed over to Gary and yanked his hat down.

Aaron, Vicky, and I all shouted for them to hurry up. But it was too late. The other teams had already finished the race while Inna was yelling at Gary.

Gary apologized on the way back to our tent. "Arrr, I really thought I saw the White Skeleton Monkey that time," he mumbled.

"I TOLD YOU NEVER TO MENTION THAT MONKEY AGAIN!" Inna shouted. She was super-steamed about her dress. But she was also steamed about Gary's false alarms. He'd told us twice that he'd seen the White Skeleton Monkey. Both times, it turned out to be a fib. "I don't need you to scare me for no reason," Inna told him.

"Arrr! You're both scallywags," Aaron said. "Clegg said that monkey hasn't been seen in ages, so just forget about it already!"

"But last night, I read about it in my book of pirate tales," Gary said. "It really is real!"

"Aye, so is that sneaky Robert the Kid and that slimy Two-Eyed Johnny," Vicky barked. "That's who we need to worry about!"

"Aye, Vicky's right," I said. Gary hung his head down. I didn't mean to hurt his feelings. He was my best mate and his book of pirate tales was always helpful. But winning the competition was the most important thing. "We need to focus on the games, that's all," I explained.

"Aye," Gary mumbled. "If you say so, Pete."

"Aye," I said. "Let's hurry back to the tent. We need to get Rotten Tooth to teach us how to swashbuckle before the competition tomorrow."

Then we all started to hurry faster. Thinking about swashbuckling was already starting to raise our spirits.

Chapter 7
Swashed and Buckled

"Ready, matey?" Hook-Hand Edward asked me.

I held the wooden sword as tight as I could and faced my opponent. She was the fiercest pirate I'd ever seen. She had curly red hair like fire.

"Ready," I squeaked.

I really wished Rotten Tooth had taught us something the night before! But when we got back to the tent, he was already snoozing in a hammock.

We woke him up.

He didn't like that one bit. "ARRR! THE NEXT MANGY PUP THAT WAKES ME WILL BE SHARK BAIT!" he roared at us. Since none of us wanted to be shark bait, we let Aaron show us how to swashbuckle. Now, I was about to find out if he knew what he was doing.

"Arrr! Come on, Pete! You can beat her. She's only a girl!" Aaron hollered.

I saw Inna and Vicky bop him on the head. Then I got bopped on the head! Only it wasn't the girl who bopped me. I had swung the sword like Aaron showed me and I ended up bopping myself!

I had a really big ouch on my head!

I closed my eyes and tried to rub it away.

"Look out, Pete!" my friends hollered. Then . . . *SMASH!*

I was knocked right off my feet.

Hook-Hand Edward held up the girl's hand to let everyone know she was the winner.

"Blimey! You got beat by a girl!" Aaron laughed. Then it was his turn to face her.

Aaron jumped around and swung the wooden sword all over the place. The girl just watched him. Finally, Aaron was completely out of breath. That's when

she went over to him and gave him a little
shove. Aaron collapsed like a soggy sail!

"Way to go, blabber guts!" Vicky giggled.

But she, Inna, and Gary didn't do much
better. They all lost their matches, too.

Our team didn't even win a single
swashbuckling match!

"Arrr! I'm sorry, mates. I had no idea

swashbuckling would be so hard," Aaron said after all the matches were over.

But none of us blamed Aaron for showing us the wrong way to swashbuckle. He was only trying his best to help.

"Arrr, I blame Rotten Tooth," Vicky said.

"Aye!" we all agreed.

"When we get back to the *Sea Rat*, I think we should tell Captain Stinky Beard," Inna said. "When he hears what happened to us today, he'll make Rotten Tooth teach us how to swashbuckle."

"Aye! But that won't help us here at Camp Buccaneer," Vicky grumbled.

"Arrr! We're never going to win now!" Aaron groaned.

"Aye," Inna and Gary agreed.

They were even dumpier than before, but I wasn't ready to give up just yet.

"Stow that talk!" I said. "There's still the treasure hunt competition, and we're the best treasure hunters around! We found the treasure at Snake Island, remember?"

"Aye," Gary said. "We even found that

treasure that made the entire crew seasick."

Inna held her stomach and made a
face like she was sickish. "Arrr, I think
we should try to forget about that one,"
she said. "Just thinking about it makes
me icky sicky."

"Aye, but it's still a true fact that we're
tip-top treasure hunters," I told my friends.
"And if we find the treasure first, there's
still a chance for us to come in first place."

"Aye?" Gary asked.

"Aye!" I said. "There'll be plenty of time
to deal with that lazy guts Rotten Tooth
after we leave Camp Buccaneer. For now,
let's keep trying our best!"

Then we all put our hands into a circle
and gave our pirate cheer.

"SWASHBUCKLING, SAILING,
FINDING TREASURE, TOO! BECOMING
PIRATES IS WHAT WE WANT TO DO!"

We raced toward the beach. Hook-Hand
Edward was waiting with a treasure map for
each team. There was no way we were going
to lose this time!

Chapter 8
Treasure Trap!

"Are you sure we're going the right way?" Aaron asked. The path had vanished and we were right in the middle of a jungle.

Inna lifted her safari hat and looked at the map again.

"I'm sure," she said. "The treasure should be straight ahead."

Inna was the best map reader at Pirate School. If she was sure, I believed her.

I marched straight through the bushes. Then . . . *SWOOP!*

My legs were swept right off the ground. So were Aaron's and Inna's. The three of us were caught in a giant net, dangling above the ground.

"Shark's fins!" Vicky cried out. "How did that happen?"

"Arrr! This time, I didn't even do anything," Gary said before anyone could blame him.

They stared up at us and we stared down. We were absolutely, positively TRAPPED!

"Blimey, are you going stand there or are you going to get us out of here?" Aaron hollered.

"Arrr! I'd like to leave *you* up there!" Vicky hollered back.

I rolled my eyes. "This is no time for arguing," I said. "You guys have to think of something, quick."

"Aye," Inna said. "The other teams are probably right in our wake."

"Aye," Vicky said, and made a serious face. She squinted and scratched her head.

Gary reached under his pirate hat and scratched his head, too. I would've scratched mine, but my hands were caught between Inna and Aaron.

Finally, Gary raised his hand in the air. "Avast, I got it!" he called out. "I heard a pirate tale once where a pirate was trapped in a net and he chewed through the ropes. All you have to do is bite a hole in the net!"

"Are you daft?" Inna asked. "There is NO WAY I'm going to chew on that dirty, slimy rope!"

"Arrr! I'll do it!" Aaron roared.

I could see him out of the corner of my eye. He opened his mouth really wide.

Then he chomped down on the rope!

His eyes went all big. Then he opened his mouth and stuck out his tongue. "YUCK!" he yelled.

"I think we need another plan."

All of a sudden, the bushes nearby erupted in laughter. We all turned to look. Robert the Kid and Two-Eyed Johnny stumbled out, laughing harder than ever.

"Arrr! It looks like our trap worked. Ye runts aren't going to win now," Robert the Kid said.

"Aye! Ye look to be *stuck* in second place," Two-Eyed Johnny added. Then they both laughed all over again.

Vicky was so angry, her face turned bright red. She curled her hands into two fists and stomped her foot down. "You two are BIG FAT CHEATERS!" she shouted.

Robert the Kid smiled. "You mean big fat *winners*!" he said back to her. Then he pushed aside a few big bushes.

There it was!

A wooden trunk filled with golden, shiny treasure!

Chapter 9
To Help or Not to Help?

"Arrr, we can't just hang around here while they take the treasure," Aaron growled.

We could see Robert and Johnny scooping up treasure in their greedy paws. They were even dancing around and singing a little bit. They were rotten sports. Plus, I didn't think it was very piratey, either!

I tugged at the net. It wouldn't budge.

"I don't think we have a choice," I mumbled.

"Arrr! The worst part is that they're going to get away with it," Inna cried. "It's just not fair!"

"Aye," Vicky said below us.

"Aye, but don't worry," Gary said. "I'll have you down in a jiffy." Then he started to climb the tree. I shouted for him to stop. Gary's not the best climber and I didn't want him to get an ouch.

"Go get Rotten Tooth. Maybe he'll *finally* help us this time," Aaron said.

"Aye, that's not a bad idea," Vicky said.

"Arrr, I can make it!" Gary said.

I peeked down. He was halfway up the tree.

But just then . . . there was a great big giant *CRASH*!

To my surprise, it wasn't Gary who fell. It was us!

Me, Inna, and Aaron plopped to the ground with a loud *thump*!

The net fell open and we all sat there rubbing our heads.

"Sink me, Gary! You could've warned us," Aaron said.

"Aye!" Inna said, brushing the dirt off her dress. "When you climb down here, you're going to get it right on the head!"

"Arrr, it wasn't me!" Gary said.

I looked up. Gary was still only halfway up the tree.

"If you didn't get us down, who did?" I asked.

Gary pointed in the direction behind me. His timbers were shaking and shivering. "He did!" Gary shouted. "But I'm not going to say his name or Inna's going to pull my hat down again."

I spun right around and looked.

I couldn't believe my eyes!

Standing right there was a monkey bigger than me! And this monkey wasn't even a real monkey. It was just the skeleton of a monkey!

"Leaping dolphins! It's the White Skeleton Monkey!" I shouted. Aaron and Vicky turned to look. Inna covered her eyes and hid behind me instead of looking.

"Aye, it jumped out of the tree," Gary said as he slid down the trunk. "It landed smack down on the branch you mates were tied to and snapped it in half!"

"Blimey! But why didn't it attack us?" Aaron asked.

"Arrr! Because it's attacking them!" Gary shouted.

The White Skeleton Monkey was chasing  after Robert the Kid and Two-Eyed Johnny.

"It must have been guarding the treasure," Vicky said.

"Aye, then it's a good thing we didn't find it first," Aaron said.

"Arrr, but we've got to help them," I said.

My friends looked at me like my brain had gone overboard.

Inna folded her arms and made a huff. "No way," she said.

"Aye, double no way," Vicky said.

"But it's in the pirate code," I told them. "We have to help other pirates in danger."

"Those aren't pirates. They're cheaters," Inna huffed.

I knew we had to help them, even if they were rotten. I had one last chance to convince my mates.

"If we help them, I'm sure we'd win the Camp Buccaneer competition," I said. "That means treasure for all of us!"

"Swords, too?" Aaron asked, and I nodded. "Arrr, then what are we waiting for?"

"Aye, Pete's right!" Vicky said.

"Aye aye!" Gary said.

Inna made a grumpy face. "Arrr, do you think there's any jewelry in that treasure?" I nodded up and down and down and up. "Okay, I'll help," she said. Inna loved jewelry even more than she hated cheaters!

"That's the spirit, mateys!" I said. "Now

everyone grab onto the net and let's hurry over to those rocks."

We grabbed the net and rushed over to the tall rocks near the treasure chest. We climbed up to the top and spread the net out like a sail. Then we each tied a stone to the end of the net.

Robert the Kid and Two-Eyed Johnny were still being chased. They were running around in circles and screaming like pirate babies. I had to remember to tease them about it once we'd saved them.

"What do we do next, Pete?" Gary asked.

"Here's the plan," I explained. "When they run by this way again, we drop the net on that monkey's head. It'll be trapped long enough for us all to get away before it can turn us into skeletons!"

"Good plan," Vicky said.

"Aye, now everyone get ready!" I said.

Robert the Kid and Two-Eyed Johnny rushed by below us. Then we heard the screech of the White Skeleton Monkey.

"Now!" I shouted, and we dropped the net right on top of him!

I GULPED as it screeched and squirmed. It sure was one gruesome ghoul!

Robert the Kid glanced up at us.

We smiled real proudly and waited for him to thank us.

"Thanks, runts!" he shouted up. "Now we can grab the treasure and win the competition!"

"Aye, thanks!" Two-Eyed Johnny shouted.

"Arrr! That's no fair!" Inna shouted.

"ARRR! No one ever said pirates were fair!" Robert shouted. "Especially pirates sailing under Captain Black Heart Robert!"

By the time we climbed down from the rocks, they were gone and so was the treasure. There was no way around it. We'd lost.

Chapter 10
So Long, Camp

"Arrr! Congratulations, mateys!" Hook-Hand Edward said. Then he awarded Robert the Kid and Two-Eyed Johnny the treasure for winning the Camp Buccaneer competition for the fifth year in a row.

"Arrr, they'd both be skeletons by now if it wasn't for us," I growled.

"Aye," Vicky said. Then she pinched her nose. "That team stinks!"

"Aye," Gary said. "This whole place stinks."

"Aye, Camp Stinkaroo is what they should call it," Aaron moaned.

"Arrr, speaking of stinking, look who's coming," Inna said. She pointed toward the beach, where Rotten Tooth was heading toward us.

"ARRR! Time to ship out!" he roared.

No one made a peep as we rowed back to the *Sea Rat*. We were still quiet when we climbed on deck. It wasn't until Captain Stinky Beard asked us for a report that any of us opened our mouths.

"Arrr, Cap'n. We didn't win," I reported. Then I hung my head down and made a frown.

Captain Stinky Beard smiled. Only I didn't see anything smiley about losing. But then he patted us on the heads. "Ye did a fine job," he told us.

"Arrr! They certainly did not do a fine job, if you don't mind me saying, Cap'n," Rotten Tooth interrupted. We all turned to face him. I saw steam coming from Aaron and Vicky's ears. Inna's face had turned bright red. And Gary was so mad, his glasses had fogged up!

I shook my head. My ears must have been waterlogged, because I couldn't believe what I was hearing. Rotten Tooth didn't do his duty and now he was trying to blame us!

"Aye?" Captain Stinky Beard asked.

"Gully fluff!" I hollered.

"Aye, 'tis true, Cap'n," Rotten Tooth said. "They didn't do a fine job. They did an outstanding job!"

I thought for sure my ears were water-logged that time!

"Aye?" I asked. Rotten Tooth had never, ever said a nice thing about us before.

"AYE!" Rotten Tooth said. "Ye sprogs didn't think I was paying attention, but I was watching ye the whole time."

Vicky squinted her eyes. She didn't quite believe him. "If you were watching us, why didn't you help us?"

"Arrr, I wanted to see what ye could do by yourselves," Rotten Tooth said. "Sort of like a Pirate School test. And ye all passed. Besides, if I helped ye, it would've been cheating."

Then he went on to tell Captain Stinky Beard and the rest of the crew how heroic we were. He told them how we saved Robert and Johnny even though they were scoundrels.

"Then, these here shipmates netted the White Skeleton Monkey all by themselves," Rotten Tooth said. "I be mighty proud of ye."

We smiled really wide.

"Aye! You did well not to sink to the level of Black Heart Robert's crew!" Captain Stinky Beard said.

The whole crew cheered.

"Hip, hip, hooray! Three cheers for our little shipmates!"

We were happy as clams after that! It was almost better than winning the Camp Buccaneer competition.

Soon, the *Sea Rat* set sail. The crew went back to work, but we stayed on the deck to watch Camp Buccaneer drift into the sunset.

As the ship picked up speed, Rotten Tooth joined us.

"Rotten Tooth? I have a question," Gary said. "If you were watching the whole time, why didn't you tell Hook-Hand Edward that Robert and Johnny cheated?"

"Aye, good question," Vicky said.

"Aye!" the rest of us agreed.

"Arrr, I'm not one for tattling," Rotten Tooth said. "Besides, ye lot will win next year."

Then he started to laugh. We all wrinkled our foreheads and stared at him. Sometimes, Rotten Tooth sure was one strange pirate.

"What's so funny?" Inna asked.

"Arrr," Rotten Tooth said. "I said I wasn't one for tattling, but revenge is another story. While ye mates were on the beach, I snuck away with that White Skeleton Monkey."

"Aye?" we asked.

"Aye!" Rotten Tooth said.

"Where to?" I asked.

Rotten Tooth didn't say anything. He just pointed out to sea. We could see another boat sailing in the distance. It was Black Heart Robert's boat.

"You snuck that monkey onto their ship?" Aaron asked in surprise.

Rotten Tooth smiled wide enough to show his green teeth. "Arrr, let's just say

there be a stowaway aboard. I don't think those two cheaters will be getting much rest tonight."

Then we all started to giggle, even Rotten Tooth!

We were all very happy. We might not have won the competition, but we were still winners. And maybe, just maybe, Rotten Tooth would teach us how to swashbuckle the next day during Pirate School.